Well-Seasoned

Well...

Kit Kyndall

Published by Amourisa Press, 2022.

Blurb

TWENTY YEARS AGO, ELLIE gave up a promising culinary career to raise her kids while her now ex-husband skyrocketed to fame and fortune with a string of restaurants she helped him build. Divorce has given her a new world of possibilities, but she's not brave enough to audition for celebrity chef Ian Scott until her kids and BFF trick her into it. He offers her the job, to her surprise, and it's a struggle to keep her thoughts on work instead of her hot boss.

Twenty years ago, Ian lost his chance with Ellie before he ever really had it. Now that she's free and in front of him again, he won't waste another opportunity. He wants to nurture her culinary potential, but most of all, he wants her—body, heart, and soul. She belongs with him. She just doesn't know it yet.

The only thing hotter than the kitchen is the spark between these two mature characters. This is a sweet, steamy tale of two well-seasoned people, who find love after forty.

Chapter One

Ellie

"HEY, WATCH IT," SAID Ellie as she adroitly sidestepped the young man holding the tray to be circulated around the party. He couldn't have been much more than nineteen or twenty, placing him solidly around the age of her kids, Kip and Anna. It sent a pang through her chest as she thought about Kip thundering clumsily through the kitchen as he was wont to do. He was in his freshman year at the university and had chosen to live on campus, so she'd missed hearing him rush through the apartment like a herd of elephants the past few months.

They were in a quick-paced environment, and she didn't have time to get maudlin about her empty nest, so she turned her attention to the smoked salmon rolls she had to complete. She was lost in the zone, so she jumped in surprise when her boss and best friend, Rachel, tapped her on the arm a few minutes later. She looked up from the task of tucking salmon just right. "What?"

"You'll never guess what I heard."

Ellie shrugged. "Yeah, I probably won't." She continued her task, knowing she still had a couple hundred of those to assemble before moving on to the asparagus tarts.

"Seriously, just guess."

Ellie rolled her eyes as she looked up. "I really don't have time to play guessing games right now. I'm surprised you want to, since your company's reputation is on the line."

"This is really important, Ellie." With seriousness that brought attention to the furrows at the corners of her eyes, her friend scowled at her. "Don't you want to know? It's about you...kind of."

Ellie arched a blonde brow. "How could it be about me? I don't know any of these people." Once upon a time, she'd moved in these circles, at least occasionally, but that was before she and Darren divorced. Well before that even, because he'd stopped including her in most of his social engagements in his networking attempts as his career had skyrocketed, making him one of the top chefs in the country.

"You could though. I overheard Ian Scott talking to one of his investors. He mentioned they're going to be doing tryouts for the new sous chef at his restaurant."

In spite of herself, she was reluctantly intrigued. Of course, the image of Ian Scott came to mind, though she'd only met him a few times in passing, and that had been years ago. She remembered him as being young, driven, and dynamic, with a head full of light-brown hair, intense brown eyes, and a dazzling smile when he flashed it. "What does that have to do with me?"

"It's the restaurant he's opening for his TV show. You know, *Fantasia*?"

She looked back at her hors d'oeuvres, continuing to prepare them. "That's nice."

"It's more than nice." Rachel practically screeched the words, earning a surprised look from some of the young waiters loitering nearby as they passed off empty trays to collect new ones.

"I still don't see what it has to do with me."

"You should try out. It's more like a casting call than a cooking interview, though you have to be prepared to cook something too."

There was a tiny bit of smoked salmon left that was too small to fit into the roll, and she'd just popped it in her mouth when Rachel made the outrageous suggestion. Ellie laughed and then gasped as she choked on the bite, quickly pushing it down by chugging from the glass of ice water she'd placed strategically nearby to reach while working.

When she could breathe again, she waved a hand and shook her head. "You're out of your mind, Rachel. I'm definitely not what they're looking for. You know they'll go for someone young, intense, and rising through the ranks."

"But what if they didn't? What if they did something different, something unexpected? Don't you know it's women our age watching cooking shows?"

"That's not true. They appeal to a large demographic of people. I know I wouldn't appeal to all those people, and there's no way Ian Scott is going to give me a shot based on what experience I gained working before Darren and I got married and had kids, and then my forays into catering as your assistant."

"Why can't you just try? You know you'd be good at it, and you were totally screwed over by Darren."

Ellie wiped her hands and handed a tray to a waiting server so she could start a new platter of the salmon rolls. "That's not true. He gave me a generous settlement, not to mention child support, and he never paid that late when the kids were still minors. He's paying for their university, and I got my apartment in the divorce. When it comes to ex-husbands, I could do far worse."

Rachel let out a sigh of exasperation as she moved out of the way to avoid a collision of waiters gathering in the commercial kitchen in the private home where they were catering the event. "I mean, he just expected you to give up your career when you got pregnant."

"No, I chose to stay home with my kids," Ellie corrected her firmly, but without heat. She well-remembered growing up a latchkey kid, with two working parents, and she'd wanted to be there for her children when they were small.

Darren's career was already taking off, and though she'd had a promising one ahead of her, it had been an easy decision at the time. She didn't regret it now, though she sometimes wondered what might've been if she'd continued down her career path. She shrugged, both to dismiss the thought and Rachel's suggestion. "I appreciate you thinking of me, but there's not a chance in heck."

"You graduated top of your class at *Le Cordon Bleu*, and you apprenticed in Paris. Then you worked under a couple of big-name chefs before you and Darren made the leap to start your own restaurant. You're a contender, babe."

Ellie laughed. "I don't think so. That was twenty years ago, and they'd never give me a fair chance."

Rachel crossed her arms over her chest, and she seemed genuinely irritated. "Are you going to regret not trying?"

Ellie gave her a vague smile. "I really need to get back to this if I'm going to stay on task, Rachel. Don't you have chocolate mousse to do?"

Rachel let out a startled cry, obviously having forgotten about that, and she rushed across the kitchen to begin prepping the tiny desserts that would circle around on trays throughout the evening. Ellie smiled as she imagined showing up for the interview/casting call, but she winced when she imagined just what a disaster it would be. Still, as the evening progressed, and she lost herself in work, she couldn't entirely ignore the voice in the back of her head that sounded suspiciously like Rachel, warning her she might regret it if she didn't try.

ELLIE SKIDDED TO A halt as she came around the corner, not expecting to see any of the guests coming out the back way. She had a stack of clean trays in her hand, and the staff was busy cleaning up after the party. Before she knew it, she was pulling back so she could ease around the corner and use it to hide so she could spy on the guests. It wasn't that she was overly snoopy in general, but because he had been the topic of conversation earlier.

Ian Scott.

Her mouth went dry as she realized he was just as handsome as ever, and though he'd gained twenty years, they fit him well. He looked distinguished now, with lines at the corner of his eyes and furrows in his face that just made him sexier, especially when he smiled down at his companion.

Her lip curled in distaste when she realized his companion had to be half his age. She was smiling up at him and chatting enthusiastically, and he was looking down at her with an indulgent smile. Ellie shook her head at that, abandoning any attempts to spy on him. Not that she'd actually been spying. Perhaps she had been reconnoitering to gather data, but then she assured herself that wasn't the case either. She had no intention of trying out for the sous chef position.

Still, she gave them a wide berth as she went to the van and stacked the armload of things she was holding. She couldn't understand their conversation, but she could hear the tinkling laugh of the pretty young thing on his arm, and her lips tightened again. Apparently, he was cut from the same cloth as Darren. Maybe she was being unfair, because who would reject the possibility of being with someone half their age?

She shuddered at the thought, since half her age would be roughly the same age as her children, who were both in college. Darren's current girlfriend was five years older than Anna, and she was one of the older ones he'd been with since the divorce. She honestly didn't know what he could have in common with the young women he dated, but it was probably mostly physical in Darren's case. Most likely Ian's too. Gross.

As she swung back around, she caught a glimpse of Ian walking away with his younger date, and she shook her head. It was obvious where his tastes went, and she didn't stand a chance—as his sous chef, of course. She certainly had no other interest in him, than perhaps appreciating his physical form. She wasn't divorced not dead, and it would take someone much blinder than her not to notice how attractive he still was, if not even more attractive than he had been in his younger years.

With a chuckle to herself at her own silliness, she brushed it off and returned to the kitchen. There was still quite a bit of work left before they could all go home, and the last thing she needed to do was stand around moping about lost opportunities or passing judgment on Ian Scott's sex life.

Chapter Two

Ellie

"THANKS AGAIN FOR LUNCH, kids." When Anna and Kip had called to invite her, Ellie had expected to be the one to pay. Instead, they'd treated her to one of her favorite Japanese restaurants, and now they were walking through the Downtown restaurant district. The Vegas air was hot and oppressive, but she was used to it, having lived more there half her life.

She and Darren had made the move to Vegas twenty-two years ago before deciding to open their first restaurant together. It had been a bustling culinary scene, and that hadn't changed. It was one of the few cities where chefs were on billboards alongside celebrities and sports figures. They weren't currently on the Strip, but there was still a concentration of nice, high-end restaurants around them, and she fretted once again that the kids had overextended their budgets. "Are you sure you don't want me to pay you back for lunch, or at least my part?"

Anna and Kip shared a glance and grinned. "Mom, you do know Dad gives us allowances, right?" Anna chuckled. "We might as well spend it as foolishly as we wish."

Ellie hesitated, wanting to chastise them, simply because she wanted them to practice fiscal responsibility, but she held back. They were good kids, and she was reasonably confident they weren't overextending themselves. If they were, their father could certainly afford to bail them out.

With the nice settlement he'd given her, currently collecting interest in the bank because she was still a little angry and didn't want to spend any of it, she could bail them out as well if the need arose. It wasn't like she hadn't earned that money, especially since she had put in tons of free hours working alongside him during the early years of their first restaurant, and even into the toddler years of their kids. He had been the one to push her out, though it had been a gradual and slow thing. Still, she knew he wouldn't have been as successful as he was without her, so she'd taken the settlement. That didn't mean she could bring herself to spend it yet though.

"Oh, let's go in here," said Anna. She was already holding Ellie's arm and steering her inside before Ellie had a chance to see where she was leading her. She expected it to be one of the shops scattered throughout the district, but it was another restaurant.

Or at least, it would be. Right now, it was obviously in the stages of being put together. Some of the furniture had arrived, but a lot of it was still disassembled and stacked haphazardly. There was a paint crew in the corner, and someone was dealing with lighting on a chandelier.

"I don't think this is the place you thought it was," said Ellie as she grasped Anna's arm, trying to turn back to the exit.

"We're exactly where we're supposed to be," said Kip as he came to her other side, taking her free arm.

Before she knew it, her children were frog-marching her forward. "What in the world...?"

"Aunt Rachel said this is the best way." Anna seemed unrepentant as she led her through the main room into the back area.

Here, it looked more like a complete business. The restaurant was definitely getting close to opening, because everything appeared in place in the chef's dream of a kitchen. It had everything everywhere she looked. Gleaming surfaces, the newest gadgets and appliances, and stark white tile floors and walls. Her heart skipped a beat, but then her eyes narrowed. "What are you up to?" She groaned as she realized Rachel had instigated this. "Is this about the sous chef thing?"

"It sure is," said Kip as he dropped the shopping bag he'd been carrying. He'd brought it to lunch with him, but she hadn't thought much of it. Now, she gasped as he opened it to reveal a leopard-printed chef's jacket. Her name was embroidered on it. It caused a funny flip in her stomach to see "Chef Ellie" so boldly proclaimed in white thread.

She scowled. "Are you trying out?" She sure as heck wasn't.

Kip laughed. "I can barely boil water, Ma."

"I don't know what you two think you're doing, but—" She let out a startled gasp as Anna grabbed her arm, sliding the sleeve of chef's jacket over it. Kip got her other side, and before she knew it, they'd wrangled her into the coat. She glared at her kids as she took a step back. "No, I'm not doing this. I'm not going to humiliate myself in front of Ian Scott."

"Think positively. Maybe you won't embarrass yourself too much," said a familiar voice from behind her. He sounded vaguely amused.

Ellie's mouth went dry as she swallowed, turning slowly to face a man she hadn't seen in almost twenty years. She hadn't known him that well, so it was strange that she could still recognize the timbre of his voice, and even stranger that it could dampen her panties. She licked her lips as she stared at him, finally realizing she was acting like an idiot. She cleared her throat. "I apologize for wasting your time—"

Before she could turn away, Anna was behind her, prodding her forward. "Yes, we're sorry we're late," said Anna. "Kip and I will just pop out to the lobby and wait for you, Mom." She squeezed her shoulder. "Good luck."

"Break a leg or something," said Kip, and he winked. It was almost painful, because in that moment, he greatly resembled his father—the young, sweet Darren she'd fallen in love with, not the selfish player he'd become.

Her lips trembled, but she somehow managed to give her children a small smile, though her eyes promised retribution. She waited until they left before turning back, surprised to find it was just Ian, and he was staring at her without speaking. She cleared her throat. "I'm sorry. They tricked me into this. It was mostly my friend Rachel's fault though."

He still hadn't spoken, and he seemed dazed for a moment before he blinked. "Ellie Aronson?"

She blinked. "Yes, but it's Ellie Darrow now. I took back my maiden name after the divorce."

He nodded, looking away quickly. There was a clipboard on the counter nearby, and he rushed over to it. He seemed to be busying himself for a moment, and then he cleared his throat. "I remember you. You kinda disappeared from the restaurant scene after Darren married you and hid you away."

She laughed. "It wasn't quite as dramatic as that. I decided to stay home and raise the kids."

He looked up with a frown. "I remember you had a lot of potential. What have you done as a chef over the years?"

She felt self-conscious, but she couldn't really lie about it. "Mostly grilled cheese and tomato sandwiches."

He grimaced. "You put tomato on grilled cheese?"

She grinned. "It gives a nice freshness and acidity."

"Is that what you're planning to make for me today?"

Ellie blinked, suddenly realizing just how far in her children had thrown her. "Honestly, I wasn't prepared for this. They sprang it on me after Rachel put the idea in their heads. We both know I'm not what you're looking for, so I might as well save us both some time and..."

He glared at her. "You have exactly half-an-hour to wow me, so don't waste it. If you don't have a dish planned, check to see what's in the fridge. I've laid in an order of various basics, so you should be able to put something together." Without another word, he went to sit on a bench propped in the corner. It clearly didn't belong as part of the kitchen decor, so it must have been commandeered for today's tryouts.

She looked around awkwardly. "Isn't there a camera test or something?"

He waved a hand. "I really don't care so much about camera presence as I do accuracy, innovation, and creativity. I'm sure you'll look fine on camera if you manage to impress me with your cooking."

She couldn't pretend it wasn't nerve-racking to have him watch her cook as she walked over to the fridge, slowly opening it. Part of her wanted to run out screaming before shouting at her children and then Rachel for dragging her into this mess. She was frankly amazed that Ian remembered her, and that actually made it worse. She couldn't run out in a rude fashion since he knew her. If he didn't know her name or anything about her, it might've been a different story.

When he'd said he had laid in the basics, he might've exaggerated. The selections were far more than basic. She had her choice of luxuriant ingredients, and she selected duck breast, morel mushrooms, fennel, and a few other accoutrements.

She busied herself for the next twenty minutes making one of her specialty dishes. It had been on the menu at her and Darren's first restaurant, and she arranged it carefully on the plate. She had a chance to take a small bite, not wanting to serve anything that she hadn't tasted, and she realized it was missing acidity. As he approached, and she glanced at the clock, recognizing her time was over, she quickly reached for the lemon she had yet to slice. With expert speed she'd forgotten she had, she cut it, drizzled some on the dish, and handed it to Ian.

He spent a moment appraising it before he ever tasted it. He brought it close to his nose and sniffed, nodding as though he liked what he smelled. Then he set it on the counter, used a knife and fork with sparing motions, and took a single bite that encompassed everything she'd put on the plate.

She watched every moment of his interaction with the food, but she couldn't tell anything. His face went blank, and he didn't speak. As the silence lengthened, Ellie realized she must've screwed up somewhere. It tasted okay to her, but her palette wasn't nearly as refined as it used to be.

She cleared her throat and took a step back, eyeing the kitchen to find her purse where she'd dropped it on the counter. She scooped it up and nodded to Chef Scott. "Thank you for the opportunity." Without another word, she turned to rushed out, happy to see her kids a moment later.

She snagged her arms through one of each of theirs and dragged them out onto the street, spending the next few minutes chastising them for maneuvering her into that uncomfortable position before bearing the bad news that she hadn't gotten the job. It was hardly surprising, but she couldn't pretend there wasn't at least a niggle of disappointment that she hadn't been able to impress Chef Scott.

Chapter Three

Ian

HE KNEW HE WAS SUPPOSED to be watching her cook, but he couldn't seem to look away from her delicious curves. Ellie had changed in the ensuing years, growing a little softer and rounder, but it suited her well. There were streaks of gray in her previously ash-blonde hair, but he liked that. It gave her distinction and maturity.

As he sat on the bench, which was uncomfortable by design to keep him attentive through the sous chef interviews, he couldn't help shifting every few seconds. It had little to do with how hard the word was and everything to do with how tight his pants suddenly felt.

The first sight of Ellie had overwhelmed him, and he'd barely managed to speak, let alone act in a semblance of normality. It was like twenty years hadn't passed, and he was right back where he'd been before, infatuated with a rival chef's wife and knowing it was an absolutely doomed attraction.

Back then, he had been on the shy side, and he'd been busy building his own restaurant empire. He certainly hadn't had time to finesse much time with a married woman, particularly since she'd seemed happy at the time. He'd known from the start the possessive need he felt for her was a hopeless emotion that would lead nowhere.

That hadn't kept him from semi-stalking her at times, watching from a distance whenever he saw her on the scene. As the time between her appearances grew, and she became less a part of his life, he'd been able to get over most of the infatuation, and he certainly hadn't expected it to come roaring back at the next meeting.

Dammit, he'd thought that was over this. When he was younger, he once thought he was in love with her, though he'd known even then that was crazy. You couldn't just fall in love with someone the moment you met them, right? Still, he couldn't help recalling the devastation he'd felt upon learning she was married to Darren. It was almost equal to the intensity of the joy he felt now upon realizing she was divorced. He must've heard it in passing, but it hadn't filtered through his brain until he was slapped upside the face with the knowledge that she was a free woman now.

A free woman who was cooking for him, and he needed to pay attention so he could fairly judge her. Truthfully, he didn't care what she served, or what it tasted like. He was ready to offer her the job just to keep her in his sphere, so he would have another chance with her. This time, maybe she'd notice him and feel the same kind of emotions that he'd felt. Still felt.

How was that possible? They had hardly been more than acquaintances in the past, and they certainly were little more than strangers now, but the caveman side of him wanted to swing her over his shoulder, march out of the restaurant, take her back to his apartment, and have his way with her. He could only imagine her outrage, and perhaps her fear, if he gave in to the urge, so he managed to pull it back.

By the time she set down the plate, he had a semblance of professionalism about him, though he was still reeling on the inside. Ian moved closer, eyeing the perfectly rendered duck fat on the duck breast and inhaling the scent. Everything was visually and aromatically appealing, so he wasn't at all surprised to find it tasted as good as it looked. When he offered her the job, there'd be no falseness about it. She'd presented one of the best dishes he'd tasted that day. Though he still had three interviews to get through, his heart and his tastebuds had already decided on her.

He blinked, abruptly realizing he was alone. What had just happened? He'd lost himself in the food for a moment, along with sensual images of consuming bites of it off her body. He cleared his throat, looking around for her. "Ellie?"

His assistant, Hammond, entered the kitchen. "How did it go?" He had a form so he could write down Ian's thoughts.

Ian scowled. "Where did she go? Where's Ellie?"

Hammond frowned. "Who's Ellie?"

"The woman who just cooked for me. I want her."

"You're ready to offer her the job? What about the other three?"

Ian waved a hand. "I don't give a damn about the other three. She must've left when I didn't say anything." He cursed his clumsiness at letting her slip away. "I have to go after her. Where's her paperwork?"

"Right here." Hammond rifled through a stack of papers attached to the back of his clipboard and handed it over. "She filled out everything online."

He smiled. "I have a feeling her kids did." He looked down at the paper, and he was relieved it had all the information he needed. There was her name, address, and phone number. He reached for his cell phone before hesitating. "I have to go after her."

Hammond looked shocked. "Now? What about—"

"You handle it. Let them cook for you and take down your impressions for future openings, but I've already made up my mind."

Hammond knew him well enough not to argue. He just sighed and waved a hand. "Very well then. Do you want to wait for me to prepare the packet for the offer?"

"No, I'll get it later." The thought of having to wait any longer to see Ellie was more than he could stand.

He took off, catching a cab and directing it to her place. He couldn't have been much more than twenty minutes after her, but he regretted the twenty minutes she must've felt she hadn't been worthy of the job. He hoped he hadn't done anything to hurt her or damage the prospect of hiring her. He was savvy enough to recognize a good chef when he met one, and he absolutely wanted her to work for him. That was the least of things he wanted from her though, but he had to rein that in. He couldn't terrify her by spilling his guts and revealing all his thoughts the moment after they'd been reconciled following years of absence.

She lived in a nice apartment building, and he wasn't at all surprised to find it had a doorman and a security guard. He wanted to rush past them, but he didn't think he could get any farther than the elevator before they apprehended him. Surely, he could manage a modicum of professionalism long enough to wait for her to give permission for him to come up.

It was a surprise that she wouldn't let him up when the doorman put down the phone after speaking with her and said, "She'll be down in a minute."

Ian muttered, "Thank you," and walked over to the bank of elevators, aware of the security guard and the doorman watching him. He didn't think he screamed criminal, so why were they giving him such close scrutiny? Did they sense his quiet desperation? Had they somehow picked up on his desire to toss her over his shoulder and flee?

She stepped out of the elevator a moment later, and she'd shed the leopard-print chef's jacket. Instead, she wore a casual T-shirt, but it was snug enough to give him a good idea of the shape of her breasts, along with a tempting view of her cleavage. He cleared his throat and quickly averted his eyes, meeting her gaze. "You ran off." The words came out more accusatory than he had intended.

Her eyes widened as she took a step back. "I was just trying to make things less awkward. You really didn't have to come all this way to tell me I didn't get the job, Chef Scott. It was obvious."

He let out a low grumble. "It wasn't obvious to me. Your food was amazing, and I'm here to give you the job. I want you."

Her eyes widened, and he wondered if she was suddenly picking up more to his words than just an offer of employment. Hesitantly, she took a step closer to him as she licked her lips. Just watching her do that made his pants even tighter, and he managed to smother a groan at the last moment before it slipped past his lips.

Ellie looked uncertain. "But why? I'm well on the downside of my career, if you could even call it that. I work part-time for my friend, who owns a catering company. You could do so much better."

"I know what I want, and I want you, Ellie. When can you start?" He kept his jaw tight and his voice implacable. He refused to accept a rejection for the job offer. He was trying to handle it is a strictly separate matter from what his emotions and body were driving him to do. He wanted the job to work out for her even if she didn't have any interest in a romantic relationship. He was determined to give her the chance she clearly deserved. Even if he had to fight her on it.

"Well..." She trailed off, clearly still having trepidation, but she smiled slowly. "I suppose you can always fire me if it doesn't work out, right? I don't know how photogenic I am."

He was unable to resist the urge to reach forward and push a strand of hair off her forehead and tuck it behind her ear. He didn't think he imagined her minor shiver at his touch. "I think you're gorgeous. The camera will love you."

Her eyes widened, and her lips parted. There was a light flush on her cheeks, and it took everything he had not to bend his head and kiss her right then. The last thing he wanted to do was blow everything with his inability to control himself, so he held himself in check.

After getting her agreement to show up for work the next day, he shook her hand, torturing himself with the light contact, and made himself step back. After a word of departing from with her, he turned and left her apartment building looking for another taxi. It was far too hot to walk in the summer afternoon, and he needed something that would clear his head, not further muddle his thoughts. He was determined that this time, he wouldn't waste this chance with Ellie.

Chapter Four

Ellie

BEFORE SHE KNEW IT, three weeks had flown by. It was busy, and she worked harder than she ever remembered working, even in the early days when she and Darren had been trying to start their first restaurant and make sure it succeeded.

There were failures, and at first, it was obvious the staff wasn't sure why she was there, but she tried not to let it get to her. Each time one of them berated her for a mistake, she reminded herself that Ian had chosen her for a reason. She was determined to get full benefit of this unexpected opportunity, so she endured the dressing-downs from her superiors, the sidelong looks from her peers, and the long hours that led to aching feet and a sore back.

Before she knew it, they had accepted her. It was obvious in the way they started to treat her. There were less criticisms, and the people she worked the line with were a lot more friendly. Technically, she was supposed to be the sous chef, but Hammond had started her with the line cooks. He clearly didn't share Ian's faith in her, and while it stung, she understood she had to earn her spot.

When she finished her shift that evening, her back ached as she'd grown accustomed to, and her feet hurt. She definitely needed to get better shoes, the kind that would cost hundreds of dollars, so she might have to dip into the money Darren had given her. Up until this point, she'd managed to live reasonably frugally on her own earnings and savings, since the apartment was already paid for.

She was being silly and stubborn, especially since she was certainly due a chunk of that money, having contributed to his success. With the intention of going shoe shopping, she stepped out of the restaurant and was surprised to find Ian leaning against his gold Bugatti. It almost seemed like he had been waiting for as her as he lifted a hand and waved her over. She looked around, making sure he was directing the invitation to her before she slowly proceeded. "Hello, Chef Scott."

"You're allowed to call me Ian, particularly when we're not at work."

She glanced behind her with a small smile. "We're still at work though."

He shrugged a shoulder. "Have dinner with me."

"Really?" She frowned. "Have I done something wrong? If you've decided to let me go, you don't have to be nice about it. You can treat me just like you would any other chef even though I'm old."

He scowled. "You're not old." He stood up, still giving her a light glare. "We're roughly the same age, and I prefer to think we're well-seasoned, don't you?"

She shrugged. "Perhaps, but you don't have to worry about a lawsuit or something. I'm thankful for the opportunity, and if it's over—"

He let out a heavy sigh. "You can be the most frustrating woman sometimes, Ellie. You just automatically assume I'm going to fire you because I ask you out? Maybe I want to discuss your performance, and maybe it's all good."

Her eyes widened, and she couldn't bite back an idiotic grin. "Really?"

He nodded as he opened the passenger door. "Get in."

"Okay." Ellie slid into the car, impressed by its luxuriousness, though it was a little on the small side. She much preferred her SUV, having traded up to one from a mom-minivan many years ago when they'd had the money to do so.

He joined her a moment later, and she wondered how he fit his tall frame behind the wheel, but he seemed to manage it with grace. "Top up or down?"

She blinked as she realized he was asking her about the car. For a moment, she'd had a mouth-watering image of him pulling off his shirt. She blinked and cleared her throat. "Down?" It was more of a question than an answer, but he didn't call her on that.

Within seconds, the top was down, and they were underway. The hot wind was whipping, with the sting of miniscule sand carried in it, but it was still refreshing in its way. The sun beating down on her was unpleasant, but the desert wind did mitigate it to a certain extent.

Cruising down the Boulevard, it reminded her of being young and carefree. She closed her eyes for a moment and tilted back her head, letting out a small cry when the wind caught her ponytail holder and freed her hair. She spent the next few minutes trying to collect it and keep it from flying around, and she was so preoccupied that she didn't realize he'd pulled into a private parking garage until the car was going up the ramp. She frowned as he pulled into a parking space. "Where are we?"

"We're having dinner."

She looked around and got out slowly, not waiting for him to open the door for her. He sent her an irritated look as he came around and discovered she'd already stepped out, and she smiled in apology, but she wasn't used to men behaving in such a mannerly fashion. It certainly hadn't been something Darren had ever done, and while she didn't really see the need for it, she appreciated the sentiment behind it. "What place is this?"

"My place."

She frowned as she slowly followed him to the elevator. "Your place? One of your restaurants?"

"No, my apartment. I plan to cook for you. Quid pro quo and all that, since you've cooked for me now several times."

Her eyes widened. "I have?"

He grinned as he pressed a button. The "P," of course. The doors closed as he said, "Hammond has standing orders to give me at least one thing you cook on every shift that I'm there. I have to be able to evaluate your progress, and I'd say you're progressing nicely."

"I'm glad to hear that." When the elevator door opened, she stepped off before him as he gestured for her to do so. There was only one door, since they were on the Penthouse floor, and she moved to the side so he could open it.

She wasn't surprised by the opulence. The apartment she lived in was fairly nice as well, though it had been purchased originally fifteen years ago, before she and Darren had moved to a nicer place a few years later. He hadn't sold it, instead choosing to keep it as a rental, and she had taken it in the divorce settlement.

She had to concede that even the place she'd had with Darren wasn't as nice as this one. There was understated elegance as far as the eye could see, and she was impressed, particularly as she walked over to check out the view. She could see the

Stratosphere in the distance, and it was higher than they were, but not much else was. "This is beautiful."

"I like it. What would you like to eat?"

She turned to face him. "Honestly, a chef of your caliber, Ian... I'll eat whatever you want me to put in my mouth."

His eyes took on an interested gleam, and she flushed slightly as she realized there might've been a note of suggestiveness in her words.

Before she could change her tone or lapse into an idiotic apology, he turned away from her to eye the fridge. "Do you like sole?"

"Sure." She knew she was supposed to be his guest, but she was antsy to hear his evaluation, so she moved closer. "How can I help?"

He directed her to a rack of wines, having her select one and open it. After she poured them both a glass, she asked, "Now what?"

"Now sit down at the breakfast bar and watch me work."

She did just that, and though she suspected she was supposed to be watching his prowess as a chef in the kitchen, she couldn't help admiring other parts of his anatomy a lot more. He moved with spare grace and economy of motion that read confidence and projected certainty. There were no hesitations about how to spice or when to sear. He knew everything instinctively, and it was surprisingly arousing watching him cook.

She cleared her throat and reached for her wine, hoping it would help her marshal her thoughts. "You mentioned an evaluation?"

"There's really nothing to evaluate. You're doing an outstanding job, and I've already told Hammond to start giving you more responsibilities now that we're sure you can handle the sous chef position."

She cleared her throat, accidentally choking on the wine. "Are you sure?"

He looked at her over his shoulder for a moment, giving her a chastising look. "I never say or do anything unless I'm very sure, Ellie." There was almost a note of warning in his tone.

She cleared her throat again, not sure how to respond. She felt unexpectedly tongue-tied and bashful, as though this was her first date. Not that there was anything date-like about it, of course.

Nothing date-like at all. She was practically screaming the words sarcastically in her head as she realized there was everything date-like about the evening—they were at his home, having fine wine, and he was cooking for her. That didn't exactly scream employee evaluation, and her eyes widened as she wondered if there was a second purpose for her being there.

Before she could stir herself into a frenzy of worry, or convince herself she was imagining things, he turned and placed a plate in front of her. "Would you mind taking it to the table?"

She shook her head as she got off the barstool and carried it to the table, along with her glass of wine. He followed behind, and they were soon seated across from each other. At first, she spent her time eating, moaning softly every few bites. "This is amazing."

"It is."

When she met his gaze, he didn't seem to be paying attention to the food. He was looking straight at her with hunger in his gaze. Again, she didn't think it had anything to do with food, and she felt flustered. She started waving hand in front of her face, wondering if she was having a hot flash. What inopportune timing. It could've been the wine too, since it always made her feel flushed, but she suspected it was something far different and baser.

Desire.

It had been a while since she'd truly felt it, and it was suddenly roaring back to life. She cleared her throat again. "Just spectacular food. Thank you for sharing this with me, Chef Scott."

"Ian." As he spoke, he reached across the table and took her hand. She'd been clutching it into a fist, but she relaxed as he started to rub his thumb across the tense muscles. "Relax."

"I am." The squeak in her tone betrayed her, and he chuckled. "Of course you are."

She swallowed heavily. Ellie was desperate to find a way to turn the conversation, but her mouth was so dry that she couldn't manage to form words. She gulped the white wine he'd opened to pair with their meal, but the crisp freshness didn't alleviate the lump in her throat.

It only grew as he continued to stroke her hand with his thumb. His circles became slower and wider, making her shiver at such a simple touch. She tried clearing her throat but was still rendered speechless.

"Your have such beautiful hands. Nimble and talented." He picked up the one he'd been stroking and examined it. He ran his thumb lightly over a scar on her thumb from a deep cut acquired during culinary school. "Scarred for your art."

She blinked, unsure how to react. When he brought her thumb to his mouth to brush a kiss against it, she could no longer pretend this was a simple meal between employer/employee or even colleagues. She halfheartedly tried to tug her hand back, but when he didn't yield it, she submitted.

Ellie gasped when he sucked her thumb into his mouth. "Ian." The word was garbled and hardly more than a guttural expulsion.

"Delicious, but I knew you would be. I want to taste every inch of you, Ellie." He stood up as he said that, holding onto her hand with a cocked brow. He was obviously seeking her permission to chase that goal.

What in the world was happening here? How had things gotten to this point? How had she missed his attraction? She'd known about her own, but she'd been so busy with her new duties that she hadn't lifted her head much. That was her only excuse.

Now that she knew, what was she going to do? She worked under Ian, so being *under* Ian posed all sorts of complications and potential problems. The smart thing to do was pull away and leave, while trying to pretend this had never happened.

With that hazy intention, she got to her feet. Somehow, when he tugged her closer, she didn't step back. Instead, she practically crashed into him, professional intentions completely forgotten.

Chapter Five

Ian

HE GROWLED LOW IN HIS throat when she was in his arms. He'd planned a leisurely seduction, but he couldn't resist taking possession of her mouth in a hungry kiss. Her tongue swept into his mouth in a bold move, and he stroked it with his own.

He didn't give her a chance to change her mind. While still kissing her, his hands framing her face as her fingers dug into the collar of his polo shirt, he maneuvered her from the kitchen and through the apartment. He didn't stop until they were in his bedroom, and he didn't give her a chance to surface or reconsider. He intended to drown any of her doubts in an onslaught of passion that allowed no room for logic or fears.

She jumped in surprise when her knees nudged his bed, but he gently pushed her down. She didn't resist, and he was attuned to even the most minute movements of her muscles, so he'd know.

He pushed her back, coming down on top of her. This wasn't the sweet seduction he'd pictured, but he was too ravenous for her. He captured her lips in another kiss, sucking her tongue into his mouth before biting gently. She moaned and arched against him before burrowing a hand in his hair to anchor him against her.

She felt so good against him. He'd imagined it so many times, but his imagination was no match for reality. How the hell had he done without her for so long? If he'd known this could be the outcome, he might have set aside his ethics and pursued her years ago.

He pushed aside the uncomfortable thought, not liking what it said about him, but unable to deny his desperate desire for the woman beneath him. He moved his mouth to nuzzle her neck, nipping lightly as she shivered and panted.

"You said something about tasting..." She sounded awkward, perhaps even a little shy, but her gaze was forthright when he tore his mouth from her neck to meet her gaze. There wasn't a hint of hesitation.

Prompted by her confidence and gentle reminder, he dipped his head and licked his way down her neck. His fingers fumbled with her buttons as his mouth explored her skin, making him feel like an inexperienced virgin in his excitement.

As though she understood that, her hands gently brushed his aside, and she dealt with the buttons. After that, he stripped off the chef's jacket to reveal a practical bra beneath. It was beige and satiny, and while it was nothing special, it was the sexiest thing he'd ever seen, because it was on her.

His fingers seemed to have regained their nimbleness, and he unfastened the front hooks of the bra to let her breast spill free. They were plump and more than a handful. He buried his face between them for a moment and breathed in the intoxicating scent of her skin. She'd worked, but she still smelt faintly of plumeria and her own natural musk. He couldn't get enough.

Yet a plump pink nipple beckoned, and he couldn't resist. He turned his head and took it in his mouth, practically devouring the bud and its surrounding areola. He moaned as she uttered a similar sound while writhing under him. He could just imagine how soaking wet her pussy was right then, and it made his cock harder than it had ever been just thinking about it.

He wanted to strip her and plunge his tongue inside her liquid heat, but he wanted to savor their first time coming together. He forced himself to slow down slightly, spending a few minutes worshipping her nipples after pushing her breasts together so he could swipe them with his tongue.

"Ian, oh..." She thrashed and arched against him.

He couldn't wait any longer. With an urgent growl, he pushed her higher up the bed while simultaneously grabbing the elastic waistband of her uniform slacks. He stripped them from her, revealing a black bikini. His mouth watered at the plump contours of her folds peeking through the lace.

He couldn't wait for a taste. Ian spread her thighs and burrowed his face into her pussy through the underwear. It provided rough friction that she clearly liked as she moaned and bucked against his head.

With an impatient motion, he ripped away the bikini to reveal her folds. She had a light dusting of blonde hair with a touch of gray, but it didn't dissuade him. He'd waited too long, and that little smattering of gray drove him wild. He pulled away to stare at her pink perfection, loving the way her nubbin barely peeked through her folds.

She shifted, clearly uncomfortable as she brought down a hand to cover herself. With a groan, he pulled back her hand and pinned it at her side. "No."

She frowned, looking embarrassed. "It's been a long time..."

He glared. "I don't want to hear about anything in your past. I can't stand to think of someone else having what's mine." Her eyes widened, but he didn't give her a chance to reply. He was afraid she might not like the possessive note in his voice, but he couldn't censor it. She was his and should have been all along.

He gave up his visual feasting that seemed to embarrass her to taste her instead. She whimpered when he plunged his tongue into her slit while pulling apart her folds with his thumbs to reveal her more fully to him. She was hot and tangy, and so wet his face was drenched in seconds. He loved that he could do that to her. It was only fair considering how aroused he was.

"Ian..." She grunted, grasping his hair and dragging him closer.

Not that he needed any prompting. He dipped his tongue inside, swiping from clit to opening as he learned her unique geography. Then he whisked his tongue gently around and across her clit, making her jump in his arms. When he dipped his tongue to her opening again, he could feel it clenching with need, clearly wanting something to fill the ache.

He pressed his tongue inside her sheath, darting in and out in a mimicry of what his dick wanted to do to her. She moaned and convulsed, her thighs tightening around him as she fucked his face with abandon. She needed more to send her over the edge.

He returned his tongue to her clit, working that sensitive area while rearranging his hands so one held her splayed, and the other sought out her wet channel. He pushed two fingers slowly inside her grasping sheath, ensuring she could take them before adding a third. As he sucked and fucked her with his mouth and fingers, her cries grew increasingly frequent and high-pitched. She had to be on the cusp of coming.

So was he, but he refused to spill himself on the bed. He pressed his cock firmly against the edge of the mattress, inflicting enough pain to regain control. Then he focused all his attention on her again, licking, sucking, and fingering her until she let out a loud moan of pleasure. Her thighs locked around his head, holding him immobile against her spasming pussy as she came. He lapped as much of her juices as he could while she rode out the extended wave of pleasure.

When she started to come down, he built her up again, wringing another orgasm from her before eliciting a third. She was sobbing and gasping by the time he let her lie against the bed in a boneless heap, eyes closed and chest rising and falling rapidly. She looked like she'd been well and truly fucked, but they weren't anywhere close to done yet.

Chapter Six

AT SOME POINT, ELLIE remembered how to breathe again. She was aware enough of her surroundings to appreciate Ian's tender motions while stripping off her socks. She'd lost her shoes somewhere along the way but didn't know when.

Then her gaze turned to him as he removed the polo with his restaurant group's logo and khaki pants. His body was still toned and taut, with a flat stomach dusted by light-brown hair that pointed in a V leading her gaze to follow down to his jutting cock. Her eyes widened at the sight.

He was big. Too big? She'd never had a cock so large, but she was up to the challenge. Realizing she was just staring without speaking, she managed to make her limp body move and sat up. When he bent down, their mouths met, and she could taste herself on his lips and tongue as she kissed him with ferocity matching his. He seemed like a starving man, and she was sure only she could sate him.

It was a heady thought, and she got to her knees, taking his arm to pull him closer. She rested her bare breasts against his lightly furred chest before wrapping her arms around him. Her hand moved down his body, and she grasped his cock.

He grunted and pulled back. "Don't."

She frowned, confused. "I want to make you feel good too."

He groaned, eyes closing. "You do, but if you touch me, I'll come all over your hand like a teenager. I've never been so turned on."

She smiled, gratified to stoke his desire to such a fever pitch. "I'll take my chances." She spoke in a sultry tone as she pushed him away and rolled onto her back. The mattress edge supported her neck, and her head hung downward. She opened her mouth and licked her lips in invitation.

He moaned as he readily accepted, guiding the cockhead to her lips. She kissed him lightly before swiping her tongue across the tip to catch a drop of cum that leaked from him. He was salty and tangy, and it was an intoxicating taste. She wanted more, so she lifted her arm behind him, cupping his ass to push him forward. She swallowed more, taking his cock inch by inch until he nestled against the back of her throat.

She moaned, realizing there was still more of him. He felt huge in her mouth, and her pussy, which should have been too satisfied to respond, twitched at the thought of feeling him inside her. She shifted restlessly as she sucked his shaft.

"Oh, god. Is there anything you don't do perfectly?" The cords in his neck bulged as he clenched his jaw. It was obviously costing him a lot to maintain control.

That was such a turn-on. It had been years since she'd had a lover with this kind of desire for her. Maybe it had been like this in the beginning with Darren, but familiarity had bred apathy for both of them, and the passion had been one of the first things to die in their marriage. It was a mistake she wouldn't make again with a future relationship.

Not that she thought the passion could dim between her and Ian if this continued. That thought brought unwelcome, intrusive questions. She had no idea what he wanted from her. Was this just a one-time event, or was it the start of something new? She banished those thoughts, not wanting practicalities to rob the magic of this moment.

She tipped her head more, taking an extra inch of him. His cock throbbed against the back of her throat, and she swallowed. That made him grunt, and he pulled away before she could stop him. "I want more." She met his gaze, watching as he held the head of his cock with intense pressure, clearly staving off his orgasm.

"So do I." He sounded rough, and he couldn't be hanging on by much more than tenacity.

She couldn't have that. She wanted him to totally lose control. With a smooth motion and barely a twinge in her back from the abrupt shift in position, she swung around and got on her hands and knees. She looked at him over her shoulder through the veil of her lashes. "Do you have protection somewhere?" She stretched toward the nightstand as she asked.

He tore past her, ripped open the drawer, and removed a condom in what had to be a speed record. Before she could do much more than tilt her buttocks in the air, he was back to her. The foil packet ripped, and his hands brushed against her nether regions as he applied the condom.

She braced herself as his fingers dug into her hips. He was jerky and uncoordinated, obviously driven beyond the bounds of all control. He wasn't capable of being gentle when he lined up his cock with her sheath, but she didn't want careful and considerate. She wanted raw and animalistic.

He practically howled his pleasure as he thrust into her with one quick push of his hips. She gasped as his length and girth filled her, accentuated by the position. It felt like too much for a moment, but she didn't ask for a reprieve. She dug her hands into the comforter and tried to hold on as he grasped her hips and pistoned in and out of her with rhythmic grunts.

Ellie didn't think he'd last long in his current state, and she hadn't expected to be able to come again already, but his cock provided delicious, firm friction against her clit through her pussy walls, pushing against the sensitive bundle of nerves with each deep, rapid thrust into her slit. She arched her hips a bit more, getting the perfect stimulation, and let out a small cry when she started to come again just a few moments later. A buzzing sound filled her brain as she surrendered to the vortex of passion.

He shouted his release, holding tightly to her hips as his cock spasmed inside her several times in quick succession. For a long moment after, they remained joined as his cock softened slowly inside her. Finally, with a sound of reluctance, he pulled away and dealt with the condom.

She heard the faucet running, and she was still trying to convince her knees, which had endured a workout they hadn't experienced in years, to move when he returned. He handed her a warm washcloth and turned to his phone on the floor. It must have fallen from his pants.

That was the buzzing sound she heard, not a consequence of her orgasm, and she almost giggled. Instead, she saved the energy for turning on her back and sitting up. The sex had been so good, she needed a stiff drink *and* an ibuprofen. She started to tell him that, but he made an ambiguous sound. She looked closer at him.

His expression was tight, and he seemed to have distanced himself. "I have to go."

She blinked, not having expected such an abrupt end to their evening. "Okay."

He looked up briefly. "We'll talk later."

She managed what she hoped was a convincing smile. "Yeah, sure." He didn't wait for her to say anything else, and he rushed away without another word. It felt like he'd abandoned her, and she wondered if that was his usual way to send home his sex partners, or if she was just special.

She blinked back tears, calling herself an idiot for getting emotional about it. Sure, the sex had been amazing, but he'd never indicated it was anything more than that. At least his hasty departure removed the need for an awkward after-conversation. He clearly wanted her to leave now that it was over, and he was offering her a graceful exit. She should be grateful.

She should be, but she wasn't. She was hurt as she dressed, and by the time she got home via Uber, she was pissed. She hadn't asked for a lifetime commitment, but even a booty call deserved to be treated with respect. Ellie wanted to unload a few unkind words in his direction, but maybe it was better to forget the whole thing and pretend it had never happened. That seemed like the smartest way to proceed, but her anger still simmered.

Chapter Seven

Ian

WHEN HE ARRIVED BACK to his penthouse, Ian was surprised to find Ellie gone. He'd thought she was going to wait for him so they could talk, but he'd rushed out without giving her much information or signaling his intention for her to stay.

He didn't even bother to drop his keys on the counter. Instead, he turned and left the apartment as soon as he entered it, returning to his Bugatti. It wasn't far to her apartment complex, but traffic was a nightmare, and he was tempted at one point to leave the Bugatti parked on the street and cover the rest of the distance by foot. With the crime rate in Vegas, he might as well hand over the keys to anyone wandering by if he did that, but his level of desperation to reach her made it temporarily seem like a viable thought.

Finally, he got to her apartment building and managed to find a parking space on the Visitor floor of the garage. When he entered the foyer a few minutes later, there was a different security guard, but the same doorman was working. He approached, trying to seem unthreatening, since he still hadn't figured out why the guy had given him the stink-eye last time he'd visited. He was getting it again, but so was the man in front of Ian waiting to talk to someone else, so maybe he just regarded all visitors like they were potential felons.

When it was his turn, he said, "I need to speak with Ellie Darrow please."

The doorman nodded, clearly remembering him. He didn't seem at all awestruck by Ian, and he hadn't last time either, so he clearly wasn't a fan or didn't recognize Ian. Ian was glad not to be recognized, especially since he wanted to see Ellie ASAP.

He expected her to come down, so it was a surprise when the doorman said, "You can go up. She lives in 14B."

He nodded his thanks and walked to the elevator, which soon conveyed him to the fourteenth floor. He felt unaccountably nervous as he stepped out and walked to her door a moment later, lifting a hand to knock. His knuckles had barely rapped against the wood before she opened the door, but she didn't invite him in.

She wedged her body to keep him from entering, giving an unwelcoming impression. Her remote expression also painted a picture, and he groaned softly under his breath as he realized in his hasty departure upon getting the text message for the crisis at the restaurant that he hadn't given her enough information to explain why he was leaving so quickly. She must've interpreted it as him wanting her to leave without fuss after they'd had sex. He cleared his throat and shifted slightly. "May I come in?"

For a moment, she looked stone-faced, and he expected her to slam the door. It was a surprise when she took a step back instead, giving him a quick gesture of permission to step inside. It wasn't the hand kind of gesture he'd expected based on her demeanor, so he heaved a sigh of relief as he crossed the threshold.

She closed the door behind them, locking it. She seemed not to want him in her apartment, but he ignored that. He ventured from the foyer and entered the living room. It was comfortable and elegant, and it felt warm and inviting, just like Ellie's personality.

He didn't wait for an invitation to sit, expecting he probably wouldn't get one. Instead, he sat on the couch and said, "You were gone when I got back."

She frowned down at him, clearly determined to remain aloof and stubborn. "You seemed to want it that way. We'd barely finished before you were rushing out."

"I'm sorry. There was a kitchen fire at *Córdoba*."

Her eyes widened, and he saw the first sign of cracking in her stony defense. Her arms loosened slightly as she frowned. "Is everyone all right?"

"One of the line cooks had to go to the hospital for smoke inhalation, but the damage was mostly to the restaurant, and we have good insurance. Still, I had to be on the scene to deal with it."

She nodded, and she finally relaxed enough to take a step back and sit down in the chair near him. He'd hoped she would sit beside him on the couch, but she didn't. He told himself it was some progress and didn't push her to join him. "I guess we should talk about what happened."

She seemed defensive as she curled up in the chair, her posture and manner radiating self-protection. "It was just a one-off thing. Neither one of us expected it."

He laughed. "Not only did I expect it, I hoped for it, schemed for it, and outright planned to get you into my place and my bed tonight, Ellie. That's where I've wanted you for years, and it's where I firmly believe you belong."

Her mouth dropped open, and he'd clearly shocked her. "What?"

He had expected it to be hard to bare his emotions and open himself to vulnerability, but it was surprisingly easy. He kicked back, putting his feet on the coffee table. "Yep. I planned it all." She opened her mouth, looking offended. He raised a hand. "Before you get your knickers in a twist, I didn't give you the job just to seduce you. I would have given you the job either way, but I fully intended for what happened tonight to happen from the instant I saw you again."

She was blinking now, clearly having trouble grasping his words. "I... that makes no sense. Why?"

"Do you believe in love at first sight?"

She scoffed. "Of course not. Maybe when I was younger, but I'm too experienced for that sort of thing now."

He shrugged. "Maybe I'm not. I think I fell at least half in love with you the first night I ever saw you. You were with Darren, and we were launching a restaurant. I don't even remember all the details now, but I was still the executive chef and not the owner then."

"*Segue*," she said softly, clearly remembering the event he referenced. She seemed discomfited that she remembered their first meeting all these years later.

He nodded his agreement as he grinned, taking that as a good sign that he'd made some kind of impression on her back then. "That was the restaurant. The owner had invited a select group of chefs who were up-and-coming, because he wanted to impress us all with his success and good taste. I remember seeing you from across the room, and you took my breath away. I wanted to get closer to meet you, but then Darren came and put his arm around you. There was such intimacy between the two of you that I knew you were lovers. It got worse when I found out from my friend Hammond that not only were you together, but you were also married. I knew it was doomed then, but I still couldn't help being infatuated with you. I guess that faded a little bit over the years as I accepted that you were married and out of reach, and then you weren't in front of me all the time. I focused on work, but I've never had that same intensity of feeling for another woman since. It's partially why I never married."

She still didn't address his feelings, but she said, "I disappeared because Darren started to maneuver me out of the picture. His tastes broadened and his horizons expanded. He told me years after he started cheating on me that monogamy was a cliché. He just didn't bother to tell me that before he started cheating. Having me and the kids around cramped his style, especially as his career continued to grow, and he got fame and recognition. Then he got a taste for young women." There was a world of judgment in her words as her lip curled. She glared at him.

He couldn't help feeling her distaste was directed toward him, and he shifted slightly. "You seem angry with me about his taste in young women."

She shrugged. "I'm not angry. I guess I'm just disappointed. I saw you at the party with that girl who had to be half your age."

His eyes widened. "Margot?" He laughed as he shook his head.

"It doesn't matter what her name is. As long as she's fine with the situation, and you have something in common with someone who's half your age..." She trailed off with a shrug, though she was clearly still annoyed about it and disbelieving they could have anything in common.

He grinned. "Margot is my niece. She lives in Bakersfield and came especially for the party because I wanted to introduce her to some of my friends in the restaurant business. She wants to get started as a chef, but she thinks she doesn't need to go to culinary school or do it the regular way. I'm giving her a little opening into our world, but she'll soon learn she's going to have to do it all the hard way."

She flushed then and looked away. "Of course, it's not my place to make judgments..."

He laughed, unable to hide his amusement. "It might not be your place, but that didn't stop you. Admit it. You thought I was a dirty old letch."

She shrugged. "Yeah, which kind of surprised me with the amount of passion between us tonight, since I'm not a pretty young thing. I thought it was just a fluke or something."

He shook his head, his lips tightening in annoyance. "You're a very pretty woman, and it was no fluke on my part. I hope to prove that to you many times in the coming years."

Her eyes widened. "Coming *years*? Just how long do you think I plan to work for you? I plan to have my own place in the future."

He laughed. "It wouldn't surprise me if you successfully start your own restaurant next week, but that's not what I meant." He swung his legs down and moved closer, abandoning his quest to get her to join him on the couch by joining her on the chair instead.

She made a little sound of protest, but it didn't last long as he lifted her up, sat down, and settled her on his lap. "I'm talking about us and our future together." As he spoke, he curled his fingers through hers while she snuggled closer. "If I was half in love with you before, and completely there now. You're probably going to say I'm crazy, and it's way too fast, but this feels like it's been years in the making, at least for me." He gently tugged on her hair, getting her to bend back her head so he could look down at her. "I'm not expecting anything from you yet, but I hope you'll remain open to the possibilities."

"Yes, very, very open." She licked her lips, making him groan. "You can't actually fall in love with someone so quickly, can you?"

"I know how I feel. I've always been a guy who sets his mind on something and gets it. It just took me a bit longer than I expected with you, Ellie." He pressed his lips against her knuckles. "I can honestly say you were completely worth the wait."

Before she could feel maneuvered to say sentiments she might not be ready to utter, he captured her mouth in a kiss and swept her off into the bedroom. They quickly discovered their previous coming together hadn't been a fluke, and the chemistry continued to burn brightly between them. It was a long and satisfying night as he sought out to prove to her over and over again the sincerity of his words and the depths of his emotion.

Epilogue

ELLIE CAST A GLANCE around the room, ensuring everyone had a glass of champagne and seemed comfortable. She was hosting a soft launch of her own small bistro. It had taken more than two years to open, and eleven months were spent apprenticing under Ian before she decided it was time to go out on her own.

He wanted to help her every step of the way, but she refused to let him. He could be her private support, but she had to make *Ellie's* a triumph on her own. If tonight's guest list was any indication, she seemed well on her way to success.

She imagined some of the people had shown up simply because of her connection to Ian, and probably more wanted to see the beautifully ostentatious engagement ring he'd placed on her finger less than a month ago for themselves. He'd proposed over dinner to celebrate her forty-fourth birthday, and paparazzi had been waiting to swarm them when they exited the restaurant. That was par for the course for him, though reporters didn't constantly follow them. He wasn't that big of a star, to her relief.

In a good mood, she'd given them a thrill by flashing the ring, and the pictures had been in several tabloids for days after. That was the closest most people had gotten to seeing the ring though, since she'd been immersed in lastminute details before opening *Ellie's* and hadn't socialized much.

She didn't mind why they were there as long as they were all suitably impressed by the food. They would contribute to word-of-mouth, and it could only help to have these people in her corner.

She looked up as Rachel approached, smiling at her friend. "You know, I have you and the kids to thank for all this."

Rachel shook her head. "Hardly. It's all your own talent and hard work."

"No, it was you, and the two hooligans." She gestured to Kip and Anna, who came over to join them. She hugged the three of them awkwardly for a moment. "If you hadn't given me the push to get my foot in the door, I'd still be your caterer."

Rachel moaned. "Don't remind me that I've lost the best assistant I ever had due to my own selfless nature."

"I'm sure you'll find someone to replace me." She grinned at her kids. "And you two have your own special roles in all this. When you first tricked me into it, I certainly wasn't feeling thankful, but that's changed." She squeezed their hands, and they squeezed in return. "Thank you for everything you've done to help me find happiness."

"Sure, Mom. We want you to have everything you deserve." Kip gave her a clumsy side-hug before following a waiter with a tray of hors d'oeuvres. He seemed happy to escape the mushy moment.

Anna stayed around longer, clearly not feeling as emotionally awkward as her nineteen-year-old brother. "I'm so happy that it led you to Ian too, Mom. You deserve to find someone who loves you as much as he clearly does."

She couldn't help looking for him in the crowd, finding him speaking to a group of investors. They weren't her investors, since she'd finally decided to use the money from the divorce settlement to fund her restaurant. Why not pay for her own success from the seeds of her previous success?

She wasn't at the level where she needed to cultivate investors, and she didn't think her career would ever skyrocket the way Darren's had, or follow the bright path Ian's continued on, but she was happy with what she had—her own little restaurant, a loving fiancé, and two great kids along with the world's best BFF. What more could she ever want?

He caught her gaze and spoke to the group before breaking away. He came over, putting his arm around her waist as Rachel and Anna made themselves discreetly scarce. He smiled down at her before kissing her on the cheek.

She frowned. "What am I, your maiden aunt?"

He chuckled. "I don't want to embarrass you in your victorious moment."

She rolled her eyes and grasped his tie, dragging him closer for a long, satisfying kiss before letting go. He lifted his head but didn't move away. "I'd never be embarrassed. I don't care who knows how much I love you."

"True, but if you kiss me like that again, everyone is going to see just how much I want and love you *right now*. They might see it on the tables or the bar. Maybe against the wall…" He purred the last word against her ear.

She shifted as her panties grew damp. "Stop distracting me," she admonished, but with faux irritation. After all, she'd instigated the kiss.

"Sure." He grinned as he pinched her behind. "For now."

She smiled at him but forced her attention to a group approaching to speak with her. They would have later tonight and every night for the rest of their lives together to indulge in passion, so she supposed she could endure the need to behave professionally for at least the next hour or two. Knowing what her night held kept her smiling and carried her through the rest of the event.

When it was over, she and Ian didn't hold back, just like always. There was no way to keep their feelings and desire in check for long, and she was confident it would always be that way.

About Kit

KIT KYNDALL IS THE pen name *USA Today* bestselling author Kit Tunstall when writing contemporary romance. It's simply a way to separate the myriad types of stories she writes so readers know what to expect with each "author."

Join Kit's Mailing List[1] **to keep up with her new releases across all pen names.**

---

1. http://eepurl.com/bpdvb9

Did you love *Well-Seasoned*? Then you should read *Seduction*[2] by Kit Kyndall!

[3]

A game of seduction…

It's obvious to Jason that his son's girlfriend is only after the Masters' money. He figures it will be an expensive lesson for the young man, but tries to ignore the situation despite the way Lanie makes him feel. It's only when Josh announces their engagement that Jason decides to do something to get rid of the gold-digger. Something cold and calculating, like seduce her away from her younger mark before scorning her. It's a straightforward plan, so why does she make him feel things he

---

2. https://books2read.com/u/bzap9Z

3. https://books2read.com/u/bzap9Z

hasn't since his wife died years ago? Could the infallible Masters have misjudged Lanie? Or is she simply playing him in return? Just who is seducing whom?

Also by Kit Kyndall

Kingwood Prep
Catching His Eye

Protectors
Safe Harbor
Hart & Soal

Pure Escapes
Ablaze
Out Of Bounds
Guarded
Succumb
Taking
Proposition
I'm No Saint Nick

Sage Valley
Reunion
A Second Chance

Seen
Catching His Eye, Part 1
Catching His Eye, Pt. 2
Catching His Eye, Pt. 3

SpicyShorts
Pawn
Two Cowboys for Cady
Ebony Enigma
Wrong Groom
Model Behavior
Biology Lessons
Mai Tais on the Beach
All Grown Up
SpicyShorts Bundle

Sweet Escapes
Falling For A Firefighter
Worth Waiting

Well...
Well-Seasoned

Standalone
Playing His Game
Snowbound
Student Bodies
Double Delights
Tied To You
Seduction
A Royal Pain
The Island
Submission
Falling For The Warrens
Billionaire's Baby Contract